To Brigitte S. whose friendship has touched me very deeply.
S.E.B.

This book is dedicated to children everywhere.
They should never forget that there are always times when
somewhere a little fox needs help.

a minedition book
published by Penguin Young Readers Group

Text copyright © 2006 by Brigitte Sidjanski
Illustrations copyright © 2006 by Sarah Emmanuelle Burg
Original title: Das Kleine Huhn und das Füchslein
English text translation by Kathryn Bishop
Coproduction with Michael Neugebauer Publishing Ltd., Hong Kong.
Rights arranged with "minedition" Rights and Licensing AG, Zurich, Switzerland.

Published simultaneously in Canada.
Manufactured in Hong Kong by Wide World Ltd.
Typesetting in Goudy Old Style.
Color separation by Fotoreproduzioni Grafiche, Verona, Italy.

Library of Congress Cataloging-in-Publication Data available upon request.

ISBN 0-698-40044-5
10 9 8 7 6 5 4 3 2 1
First Impression

For more information please visit our website: www.minedition.com

Little Chicken

Brigitte Sidjanski & Sarah Emmanuelle Burg

Little Fox

minedition

Little Chicken had played in the snow all day. That evening she was
so tired she snuggled deep down in her warm nest to go to sleep.
Suddenly there was tapping at the door.
"Who's there?" asked Little Chicken.
"It's me, and I..I...I'm freezing. I'm lost and can't find my way home.
Please let me in," said a voice from outside.

"No, no, no!" cried the other chickens, running in
all directions. "Don't let anyone in!"
"But why not?" asked Little Chicken, surprised.
"It's just a little fox."
"Just a fox!" shouted the older chickens. "Don't you
know foxes eat chickens?
Now come and help us block the door."

Soon it was quiet again,
but Little Chicken couldn't sleep.
Outside the poor little fox was freezing.
"He couldn't possibly be dangerous,"
she thought, and so...

...She jumped right out the window.

"Come on, Little Fox," whispered Little Chicken.
"I know a warm and comfy spot for you."

In the barn the cow was very surprised when she saw the unusual pair coming towards her. She said in a friendly voice,
"Little Chicken, you know what they say about foxes and chickens. But you'll be safe here. Now get some sleep."
And she kept a careful watch all night long. The next morning the two began their search for Papa and Mama Fox.

On the edge of the woods they met some wild pigs.
"Have you seen Papa and Mama Fox?"
"Foxes? No, we haven't seen any foxes," called out the wild pigs, surprised. Then one of them whispered to her, "Little Chicken, you'd better be careful and watch out for foxes. They'll eat you." But Little Chicken felt she just couldn't let Little Fox down.

A deer came out of the woods, and when he saw the two together his eyes widened.

He said, "Little Chicken, save yourself, jump up here on my antlers."

This Little Chicken did happily, but not to save herself. From high up on the deer's antlers she had a good view, but she still couldn't see either Papa or Mama Fox. However...

...she did see her friend the badger who was busy
building a snowman.
Little Chicken and Little Fox thought that looked like fun,
and started to help, when suddenly the badger shouted,
"Look out, Little Chicken! Foxes are coming."

"We've finally found you!" said Papa Fox joyfully. "And my goodness, what a yummy breakfast you've brought!"

"No, no Papa," said Little Fox. "The little chicken isn't breakfast! She rescued me when I was lost and freezing."

The two big foxes didn't know what to say.
Not eat a chicken — that's not the way it was supposed to be!
Then finally Mama Fox said, "Well, if she is your friend,
I guess that's different."
"Yes, that is something quite different," added Papa Fox.
"We won't eat you," he told Little Chicken.
"We promise!"

Then Little Chicken started on her way home.
Saying goodbye wasn't hard, because the two new friends
would meet again tomorrow...
AND they would build their own, even bigger snowman.